There was once a princess called Alice, who never laughed.

She never smiled the tiniest bit.

This made her father, the King, very sad.

"My poor Alice," he sighed. "How awful to live without laughter."

The King tried everything he could
think of to make her laugh…

HONK, HONK!
HONK!
Hold Tight!

Jessica Souhami

Frances Lincoln
Children's Books

For Robert, with thanks for all the laughs.

About the Story

Stories about a princess who never laughs are widespread and have been told for centuries. They are particularly well known all over Europe, and an important early version is in Basile's Neopolitan *Il Pentamerone* of the seventeenth century. The hero who makes the princess laugh is always a poor, good-hearted young man who is then offered a great prize by the king – often the princess herself as a bride. I couldn't have that! It seems more likely to me that the princess would realise how great it would be to have a funny husband and that she would propose to him! A golden goose is the magical element of the story, and magical golden birds are found in stories as far back as the fourth century BC in the *Jataka Tales* of the birth stories of Buddha.

JANETTA OTTER-BARRY BOOKS

Text and illustrations copyright © Jessica Souhami 2015

First published in Great Britain and in the USA in 2015 by Frances Lincoln Children's Books,

74-77 White Lion Street, London N1 9PF

www.franceslincoln.com

A CIP catalogue record for this book is available from the British Library.

ISBN 978-1-84780-540-9

Illustrated with collage of Ingres papers hand-painted with watercolour inks and graphite pencil

Printed in China

1 3 5 7 9 8 6 4 2

But Alice remained glum.

The King thought for a very long time
and then he announced,

"I will share my kingdom with anyone
who can make Princess Alice laugh."

Many people tried — but they all failed.

Princess Alice was still gloomy.

The news reached a poor young man called Peter,
who decided to see this glum princess for himself.

He packed a loaf of bread and a bottle of wine
and set out for the palace.

After a while he saw an old woman wrapped in a huge black cloak, sitting by the roadside. She looked tired and hungry.

"Please, sir," she asked, "can you spare a crust and a drop to drink?"

"Of course," said Peter. "Take my loaf and wine. I'm young and strong and can do without."

As soon as these words were spoken,
the old woman swept aside her cloak...

AND REVEALED...

a beautiful goose with feathers of pure **GOLD**.

"You're a kind-hearted lad, Peter," said the old woman, smiling. "Tuck this magic goose under your arm and carry it to the palace, where you will be rewarded."

"BUT," she warned, "if anyone stretches out a hand towards the goose, it will cry,

'HONK, HONK!'

and you must call,

'Hold tight!'

See what happens then!"

The old woman chuckled and disappeared!

Peter was astonished.

But he picked up the goose and went on his way.

A young woman passing by looked at the magnificent goose.

"Mmm," she said to herself. "A gold feather would look wonderful in my hat. No one would miss just one little gold feather."

She stretched out her hand to the goose's tail **AND…**

the goose cried,

"HONK, HONK!"

Peter called,

"Hold tight!"

And the young woman could not pull her hand free!
She was stuck fast to the goose and had to follow on behind Peter.

A man stretched out his hand
to help the young woman,
and guess what?

YES!

The goose cried,

"HONK, HONK!"

Peter called,

"Hold tight!"

And the man could
not pull free. He had
to follow too!

In the same way, Peter collected a baker delivering buns.
She laughed and pointed to the man and…

"HONK, HONK!"

"Hold tight!"

She was stuck.

Then a clown who reached for a bun...

"HONK, HONK!"

"Hold tight!"

A butcher's boy who
wanted a balloon...

"HONK,
HONK!"

"Hold tight!"

And a small dog who smelled sausages...

This odd chain of people and dog **scrambled and shambled** behind Peter, higgledy-piggledy all the way to the palace.

Princess Alice just happened to look out of her window as they passed. And when she saw this comical bunch...

she smiled,

she chuckled,

she laughed

until her sides ached.

And suddenly...

...the spell was broken!

The magnificent magical goose disappeared,
and the people came unstuck and scurried home.

The King was delighted.

He hugged Peter and thanked him again and again.

And so, as promised, the King shared the kingdom with Peter.

After some time, Princess Alice thought how good it
would be to have a husband who made her laugh.

"Will you marry me, Peter?" she asked.
And Peter said,

"Yes!"

And they lived merrily ever after.